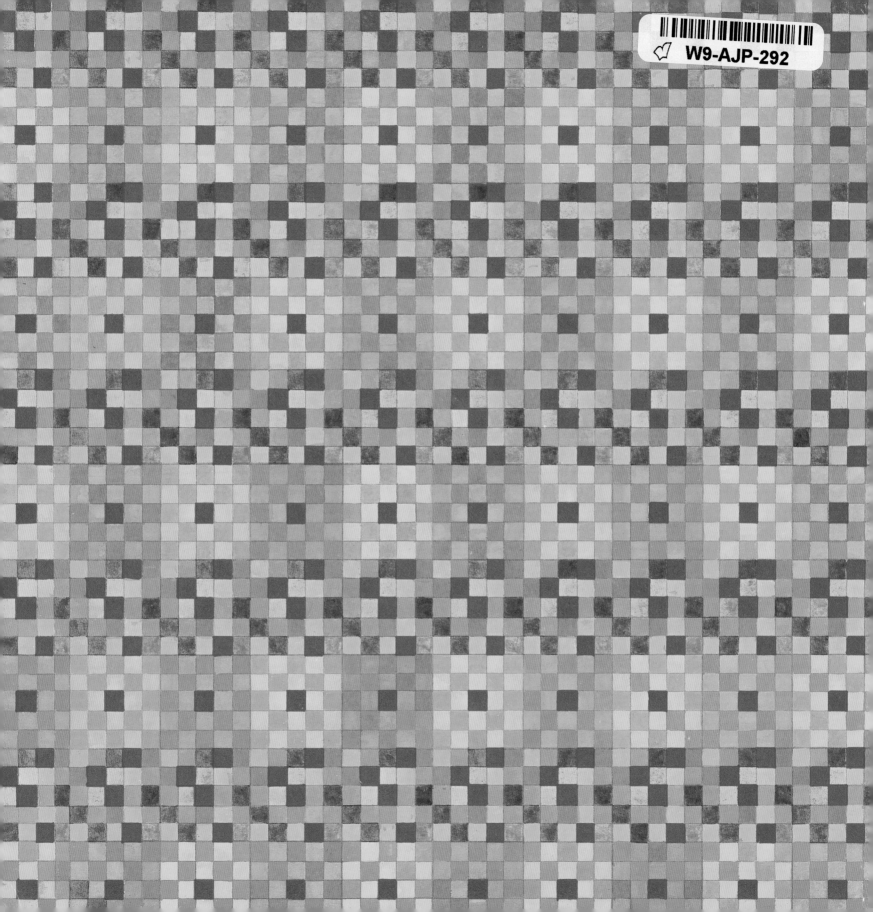

FOR "MRS P."
I.B.

FOR MARGARET FREE
N.P.

FIRST U.S. EDITION

ISBN 0-316-70521-7

LIBRARY OF CONGRESS CATALOG CARD NUMBER 93-80446

10 9 8 7 6 5 4 3 2 1

CONCEIVED, DESIGNED, AND PRODUCED BY THE ALBION PRESS LTD.,
SPRING HILL, IDBURY, OXFORDSHIRE OX7 6RU, ENGLAND

PUBLISHED SIMULTANEOUSLY IN CANADA AND ENGLAND BY
LITTLE, BROWN & COMPANY (CANADA) LIMITED AND
LITTLE, BROWN AND COMPANY (UK) LIMITED

PRINTED IN ITALY

KING MIDAS

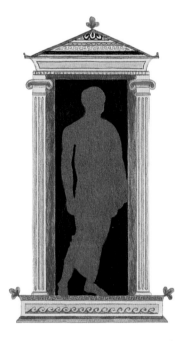

RETOLD BY
NEIL PHILIP

ILLUSTRATED BY
ISABELLE BRENT

LITTLE, BROWN AND COMPANY
BOSTON · NEW YORK · TORONTO · LONDON

ALL MEN DREAM OF RICHES WITHOUT END. YET DREAMS CAN BETRAY, AS KING MIDAS FOUND TO HIS COST.

MIDAS WAS ONLY A BABY IN HIS CRADLE WHEN HIS FORTUNE WAS FIRST FORETOLD. AS HE LAY SLEEPING, THE ANTS OF THE COUNTRYSIDE WERE SEEN FERRYING GOLDEN GRAINS OF WHEAT AND PLACING THEM BETWEEN HIS LIPS.

HIS OLD NURSE SAID TO ANYONE WHO WOULD LISTEN, "MARK MY WORDS. THIS CHILD WAS BORN TO GREATNESS. HE WILL BE THE RICHEST MAN IN ALL THE WORLD."

Midas became king of the land where he was born, and he ruled it wisely and well. He was rich in nothing more than the respect of his people and the love of his wife and child. His greatest treasure was his rose garden, in which roses of all kinds grew, climbed, and rambled.

It was said that the scent of the roses was so intense it could make you faint. And that may be why the satyr Silenus, when he wandered into the garden, collapsed in a heap beneath a tree.

The gardeners found him there, slumbering in the shade, a great, fat, snoring creature with an empty wine flask at his side. Laughing, they bound him with flowers and took him to the king.

Now Midas was wise in many things, and he recognized Silenus at once as the companion of the god of wine and passion, Dionysus. So Midas feasted Silenus royally, and for ten days they ate, drank, and sang.

Sometimes Silenus capered clumsily to a tune from the musicians; sometimes he told wonderful stories.

He had been, he said, to the very edge of the world. There, even the fruits on the trees were full of magic. A bite from one would make you wither and grow old; a bite from another would turn an old man into a baby again.

The days of feasting passed in laughter and song, but all good things must come to an end. At last, Midas and Silenus set out together to seek Dionysus so that Silenus could once again join the god's company of merrymakers.

They found Dionysus musing alone by the banks of the river Pactolus. The gleeful, mischievous god was delighted to have his companion back. "One good turn deserves another," he said. "King Midas, name your heart's desire, and it shall be yours."

Who can be sure of the whims of the gods? Midas took no time for thought, but seized the offer while it was there. "Grant that everything I touch may turn to gold," he cried.

Dionysus let out a great whoop of laughter. "It is done," he said.

As King Midas walked home, he began to tremble and shake, as do all those who meet face to face with one of the immortal gods. He knew he had been more than lucky to find the god in such a generous mood, for it was said that with Dionysus light-hearted revelry could turn in a moment to violent frenzy. Midas had not dared to hope for such a wonderful gift. Yet he wondered if Dionysus's laughter meant that the god had only been making fun of him.

Idly, the king broke off a green twig from a low branch of an oak tree. As he twirled it in his fingers, he glanced down. It had turned to solid gold!

Behind him, Midas's footsteps gleamed and glinted in the earth.

Midas entered his own rose garden and apple orchards. He caressed each living, scented rose as he passed, and each turned to solid, lifeless gold. He touched all the lowest apples in the apple trees, and they began to shine like the fabled golden apples of the Hesperides.

KING MIDAS WAS FILLED WITH JOY. THE NURSE'S PROPHECY WAS FULFILLED, FOR SURELY NOW HE WOULD BE THE RICHEST MAN IN ALL THE WORLD. ANYTHING HE WANTED, HE COULD HAVE.

HE PAUSED AT THE PALACE DOORS TO BELLOW FOR A SERVANT TO WASH HIM CLEAN OF THE DUST OF THE ROAD. AS HE RESTED HIS HANDS AGAINST THE DOORS, THEY TOO TURNED TO GOLD.

THE CLEANSING WATER SPILLING ONTO KING
MIDAS'S HANDS POURED OFF THEM IN A STREAM
OF LIQUID GOLD. THE KING BEGAN TO DREAM OF
A WHOLE WORLD TURNED TO GOLD, AND HIMSELF
THE RULER OF IT.

"WE MUST CELEBRATE," HE SHOUTED. "BRING
FOOD! BRING WINE! LET US HAVE MUSIC!" AND HE
CLAPPED HIS HANDS TOGETHER IN DELIGHT.

KING MIDAS SAT DOWN AT THE TABLE TO EAT AND DRINK. HE PICKED UP A LOAF, MADE FROM THE LIVING GOLDEN GRAIN, BUT WHEN HE TOUCHED IT, IT GREW HARD. "THAT WOULD CHOKE ME," SAID THE KING.

HE BIT INTO A LAMB CHOP, HOLDING IT BY A GOLDEN BONE, BUT AS SOON AS HIS TEETH TOUCHED THE MEAT, IT TOO TURNED TO GOLD. "I CAN'T SWALLOW THAT," HE SAID.

HE PICKED UP A CUP OF WINE, DIONYSUS'S OWN DRINK, AND POURED IT STRAIGHT DOWN HIS THROAT, BUT AS IT FELL IT TURNED TO MOLTEN GOLD.

THE KING'S WIFE HEARD HIM COUGHING AND
SPLUTTERING AND RAN TO SEE WHAT WAS THE
MATTER, HOLDING THEIR CHILD IN HER ARMS.

"KEEP BACK," HE CRIED, FOR HE SAW AT LAST
THAT NO LIVING THING COULD SUFFER HIS TOUCH.
HE WAS ALONE WITH HIS HUNGER, HIS THIRST,
AND HIS EMPTY GREED.

HE PRAYED TO DIONYSUS, "O, LORD OF THE
VINES, YOU HAVE HAD YOUR JOKE. PLEASE RELEASE
ME FROM THIS TORMENT."

GREAT DIONYSUS HEARD THE KING'S PLEA AND, PITYING HIM, DECIDED TO FREE HIM FROM THE PRISON OF HIS DEADLY TOUCH.

AS KING MIDAS SLEPT, HE HEARD THE GOD'S VOICE IN HIS DREAMS. "GO BACK TO THE RIVER AND TRACE IT TO ITS SOURCE," IT SAID. "BATHE IN THE POOL WHERE THE SPRING BUBBLES UP, AND YOU WILL BE WASHED CLEAN OF THE TAINT OF GOLD."

As Midas bathed in the river pool, his power to turn things into gold flowed out of him into the river itself. That is why the river Pactolus is veined with gold to this day, and the soil of its banks gleams where the water has kissed it.

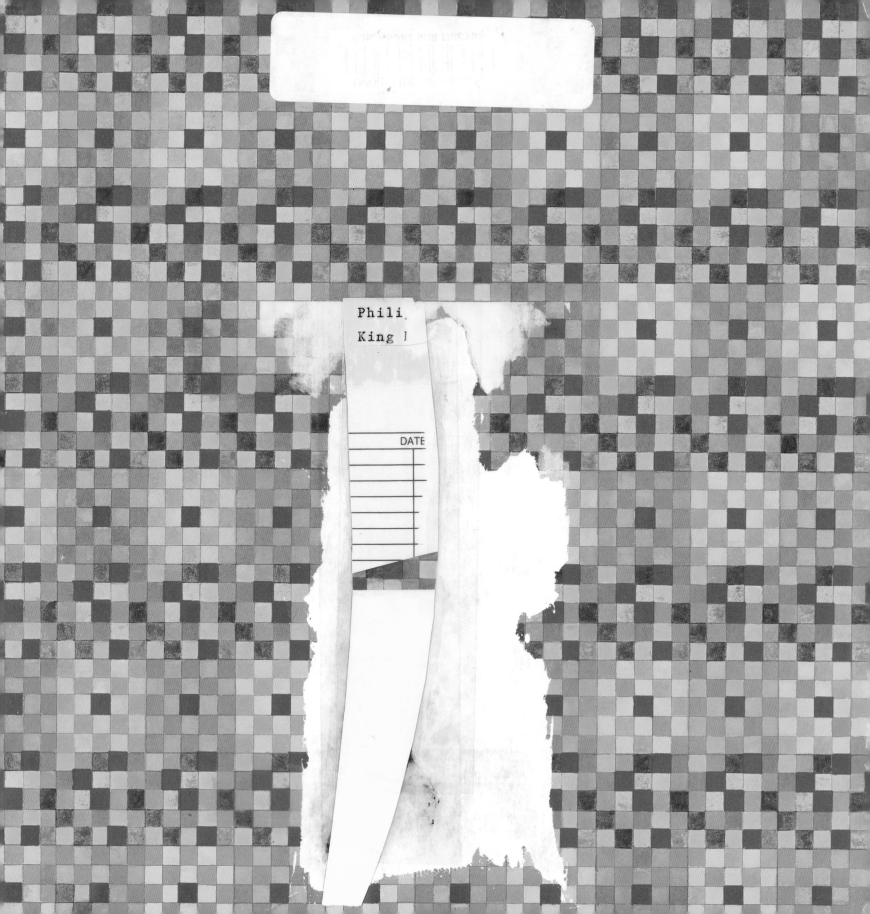

DATE